CLARE ROSKILLY

Follow Mimi's adventures as she discovers tiny fairies
behind the rockery in her garden.

Also by Clare Roskilly:

Circle of Dolphins

Diadem Books 2010   ISBN 978-1907294723

CLARE ROSKILLY

fairy world

Follow Mimi's adventures as she discovers tiny fairies
behind the rockery in her garden.

MEMOIRS
Cirencester

Published by Memoirs

MEMOIRS
PUBLISHING

25 Market Place, Cirencester, Gloucestershire, GL7 2NX
info@memoirsbooks.co.uk www.memoirspublishing.com

Fairy World

ISBN: 978-1-909304-44-4

For Sue

Thanks to Kevin Moore

Part 1

Chapter One

IT WAS CHRISTMAS and I was home again. Dad had taken me away from the magic place on top of the rock in the middle of the sea back to Brockley. He was downstairs dressed neatly in a maroon jumper and trousers. He was whistling and happy - he had brought me home. After my shower I was going to tell him everything that had happened to me at the magic place inside my mind.

I was ten years old now, but I sort of believed I'd grown up to be twenty-four. Had it all just been a dream, I asked myself? How could it have been though, because Dad had 'rescued' me and now I was his little girl again.

The garden at Brockley had a very steep rockery which was adorned with herbs and primroses and daffodils. To get to the top I had to pick my way between the plants in a zigzag motion until there was no further to climb. In the summer I would sit at the top where the view was spectacular. I could see the whole of the village including the church, because our garden was the highest in Brockley. I could even see as far as Wales, and that was where Aunt Florence lived.

Now I had had my shower, and in my nighty and dressing gown, I went downstairs to find dad cleaning out the fireplace. The Christmas tree was glinting in the corner, with tinsel and pretty lights.

"Where is the angel for the top of the tree?" I asked him.

"That angel has been my guardian angel and a great comfort to me while you were away," he said.

I searched in the decoration box but could not find her. There were just lots of ball-balls and Father Christmases with little hooks on them so they could be hung on the tree.

"But Dad," I protested, "where is she?"

Dad sat down and adjusted his trousers at the knees. He smiled a sort of sideway smile and opened his arms, gesturing to me to go to him for a hug. I could see that he wanted to try to explain to me about his guardian angel, so I went over to him, hugged him and sat on the arm of his armchair.

"I thought you wouldn't mind if I stayed with Aunty Florence forever," I said.

"No Mimi, I would not let that happen," he replied. Then he went on:

"Our Christmas tree angel flew up to my bedroom one night and I suddenly awoke to find her shining above my head. She told me that you would be home for Christmas, and it's true you are, home at last! I let you stay for a year, but to you it's been fourteen years. I don't really understand it." He hesitated. "All I know is that the angel helped me to bring you home, so I worried less. Once she said in her angelic singing voice that when you were home she would turn back to paper, and hoped to rest in a little bed, which I have made for her in this drawer."

Dad got up and went to the borough, opened the drawer and there she was—in a bed made from his hankies and a pincushion for a pillow.

"How can I be ten years old again?"

"You have not been ten before," Dad said, "you were nine last Christmas!"

"But that can't be possible Dad, because when you got to me, fourteen years had passed. I can tell you what I have been doing during these years and then you might believe me."

"I do believe it, you have been to a magical place and I'd like to hear all about it, but first let's enjoy a family Christmas. It's Christmas Eve tomorrow and Brian is coming to stay."

Then he passed me the decoration box and picked out a robin which he placed carefully on the very top of the tree. Next there was a knock at the door.

"I think it is Gregory from next door," Mum said. She looked out of the window and beckoned to him to come round to the back of the house. She didn't like opening the front door in the winter because the heat from the house would escape all at once. I walked through the kitchen which had a smell of freshly cooked mince pies in it, and a sound of Christmas carols coming from the tape cassette recorder. Mum opened the back door, and I looked out to see two feet, two legs and a big box of holly hiding a face behind it.

"I managed to get some with loads of berries," he said.

Mum smiled, took the holly from him and put a five-pound note in his little cold hand. Before I went to bed, I helped Mum cut up the holly branches and then put sprigs of it behind pictures hanging on the walls.

"In the magic place there were lots of holly berries all year," I said.

"Well, you are not there anymore, and I want you to forget it if you can," she said. She went on: "When your father found you, you were on a rock, but only because you swam out to it. You had been staying with your Aunt Florence and when Dad got to the sleepy Welsh village, she told him where to find you. You have been away for a year Mimi."

"But, Mum," I said, "it was the Christmas angel that told Dad where to look!"

"Christmas angel?"

"Yes Mum, Dad told me all about her you know, how she came to life!"

Mum picked up another sprig of holly and attached it to a candle to make a table decoration. She gave me a quizzical glance and then said:

"I expect he just wanted you to feel some excitement now it's Christmas, to see if you could forget whatever happened to you while you were away. Do you remember how you used to believe in Father Christmas?"

"Yes," I said, "and now I feel as disappointed about the angel not being real as I did about Father Christmas."

Dad walked in, having heard the conversation.

"Aunt Florence told me you had been reading magic stories about fairies a lot," he said. "She said that it was these books which made you think you'd been with her for fourteen years. She said you'd been eating berries in the garden which you'd mistaken for wild strawberries, but were actually from a completely different plant. I don't know if the berries were poisonous but the next morning she said you were distant and acting peculiar. So… I wondered if by making up a story about an angel, then you would be pleased to be home. I am sorry you felt you had to stay with Aunt Florence for a whole year."

I smiled at him and then said, "After staying for a month, I didn't want to come home. I was just so involved in her magic fairy books that I couldn't come home until I'd read them all. I do remember eating the wild berries in her garden and feeling very sick. That night I had a visitation from a real fairy who told me the fairy community was in trouble. She said that when I get home I must help the fairies that live behind the rockery and in the moss. They are so tiny that they cannot fetch enough holly berries they need for the whole year. She said I must collect as many as I can and somehow make sure the fairies get them so they would be able to make the vital berry juice which they need to drink to stay alive. So when you told me the Christmas angel had come alive, I was unsure. However, thinking back to the fairy books I have been reading all year, the actual size of a fairy is not at all as big as the Christmas tree angel that you pretended was real. The real fairies are so tiny that four of them are needed just to carry one holly berry. I have read that they cannot be seen very well at all, they are so small. And that's why I stayed away so long."

I looked up at Dad and continued, "I had to learn about fairies so I can help them, the real ones that exist behind our rockery. If they don't get holly berry juice then they will have to find another sort of berry. This could be dangerous because some are poisonous to them just as the wild berry I ate was poisonous to me. Tomorrow I shall take all of the berries off the sprigs of holly we have in the house and put them all in a jar."

Chapter Two

THERE WAS EXCITEMENT the next morning when Brian arrived. He had driven at least seventy miles with his dog whining most of the journey. Flufftuff leaped out of the car and ran right up to me, tail wagging energetically. I was holding my jar of holly berries and when he jumped up to lick my face, he knocked the jar out of my hands.

"Sorry Mimi," Brian said, stooping down to help me pick up the berries. Brian was a great family friend who was a bachelor and who always spent Christmas with us. He was tall and broad and had very dark brown curly hair. He used to work for a brewery, and that's where he became friends with Dad as they both worked there together.

"Come in and have a drink, Brian," Mum said, "I've made some *strong* mulled wine."

She emphasized the word strong because last year he had said that the mulled wine was too weak.

"I shall get the presents out of the boot first," he said. He didn't say anything to me about my year away—maybe he thought it best not to mention it in case any feathers were ruffled. He came inside with the presents and a small suitcase and a bowl and bed for Flufftuff. After chatting for a while and having a few drinks he said, "It seems Flufftuff enjoys your company so much that when we have to go he sulks for ages."

Just then as I watched Brian lift up the wineglass I considered how long *ages* meant to me.

"I get it now!" I exclaimed aloud.

"Get what?" asked Mum.

"Nothing!"

Inside my head the cogs were turning and I realised that a year to us is the equivalent of fourteen fairy years. "So that's why I believed I've been away for fourteen years!" I said.

"What do you mean?" Brian asked.

I sat down at the table with him and went into detail about how I'd found out that hundreds of fairies lived in the moss and behind our rockery. I told him that one fairy landed on my bedside table once, and said all that I had read about them was true. I don't think Brian believed me because he shook his head from side to side and said:

"But how do you know for certain that they exist when you haven't seen one?"

"Because I've been away for fourteen fairy years learning where they live, what they need to drink and how they try to help any sick flowers."

I went upstairs, away from the adults so I could think carefully about my next move. Now I'd collected the holly berries, how could I find out where to leave them for the fairies to collect? I went outside the back door and started to climb up the rockery. Some of the moss was scarce and some was in large clumps. I knelt down looking carefully for any holes that might be the door to the fairy kingdom (behind the rocks and plants). There was no hint of an entrance. I decided I'd get my jar of berries and take them up to the top of the rockery and literally pour them down the steep garden.

The next day there was no sign of the berries being found but I noticed a robin at the left side of the rockery with a twig in his beak. I thought back to one of the fairy books I had read which said that a robin was always a sign that fairies were nearby.

Suddenly I felt an itch on my nose, and remembered not to scratch it in case a fairy had landed there. I so much wanted to see a real one, and I had an idea how to. I walked very slowly to the back door and into the kitchen and then through to the sitting room. Then, still moving steadily and stealthily I opened a drawer, rummaged around and found what I was looking for. It was a magnifying glass. I put it on the top of my nose next to my eyes and I couldn't believe what I saw—a tiny little thing with delicate butterfly wings! She was wearing a little orange dress which looked to me was made from primrose petals.

"Have you come to help us, dear sweet girl of the rockery?" I thought I'd imagined a voice, but no, I had actually heard the fairy speak to me.

Then it came back to me, and I remembered why I had eaten the poisonous berries, (not the holly berries; the other ones) in Aunt Florence's garden. Her magic book had explained that any child that loved fairies, who ate a strange fruit, would be able to hear the fairies speak. Her voice was gentle but squeaky, a bit like a child's voice. She said that the doorway into the kingdom had been blocked up with rabbit droppings, which had frozen over in the December weather. Then she said if I got a trowel then I could dig a hole and renew the entrance. She asked if I'd go for a walk to the woods also, where there was lots more holly to be found. I put on a thick coat and wellies, and set off. She told me in my ear that I would be her best friend in the whole world if I did this. I could even hear her as I trampled through the leaves and edged around muddy patches along the woodland path. I found lots of holly and picked off the berries and put them in the rucksack I was carrying.

"We only need the berries, not the leaves, and enough to live on until next winter," she said.

"Can you make use of the leaves too for something?" I asked.

"We do make use of softer leaves for bedding but holly has sharp points on them which have been known to hurt us before." She went on to say that one fairy had flown right into a holly spike when trying with the others to pick a berry, and she had died. "Then," she said, "the rest of the fairies became fearful of holly leaves and so we all hoped a human girl would help one day. While flying around we'd talk amongst ourselves of the little girl playing with her dolls outside and of the boy next door also. We saw your nimble fingers, and imagined how easy it would be for you to pick berries for us."

"Well, now I know your problem," I said, "I'm going to collect as many as I can here, and I shall gather together all the holly berries I scattered over the rockery too—ouch!" A holly spike had pricked my thumb through my glove.

"Are you alright Mimi?" asked the fairy with concern.

"Yes, oh here's Flufftuff!" He had followed me into the woods and was now jumping up at me trying to lick my face. He started barking and running circles around me and I thought how I'd just gone off on my own without telling Mum or Dad where I was going, and that they could be worried about me. "Come on," I said, "let's go home."

The fairy said she would hold on to me and have a lift back to the rockery.

"Where have you been, Mimi?" asked Dad when I got home. "It's Christmas day tomorrow; have something to eat and then go to bed, please."

I ate some chicken and mushroom pie, and drank some blackcurrant juice, then went upstairs to my bedroom. I'd have to finish collecting the berries on the rockery tomorrow morning, it's too late now, I told myself.

Chapter Three

THE NEXT MORNING I felt a weight on my feet when I awoke. Looking at the end of my bed I saw a stocking bulging with presents.

"Are you still there, fairy?"

I wanted to know if she had been there all night. Then 1 heard her:

"Yes, precious girl who is helping us, yes I've been watching you, and I watched as your mum brought in your stocking too."

I unwrapped each present one by one, enchanted by the gifts Father Christmas had given for me. At the end of the stocking was a tangerine and a walnut, and a shiny coin.

"It's Christmas everyone!" Brian's voice travelled upstairs and into my bedroom. Next, Flufftuff started barking and there was a sudden crash. It was just like Brian to get his dog over excited; it happened every year. Flufftuff had knocked a special plate off the small table in the hall.

"It's okay," I heard Dad say, "I never liked that particular plate anyway."

After getting dressed quickly I ran downstairs into the kitchen. Dad was busy basting the turkey while Mum was making stuffing, humming away as she did it. I went outside to the shed where the garden tools were kept and picked up a small trowel.

"Just go up the rockery on the left-hand side until you find a funny shaped stone near a big clump of moss," said the fairy in my ear.

I found the stone, and then dug away the rabbit droppings. Eventually I found a tiny golden door which had not been uncovered for eleven fairy years. This was a long time to be unable to use the door to the fairy kingdom.

"We had to find another way in," said the fairy, "it was not easy to do. When your dad planted some tulip bulbs we found a crack in the rockery which was big enough for us to get through, but too small for the vital berries we need. We had to crush the berries before bringing them into our home and we did this to each and every one of them and collected the juice in little jars. I haven't told you my name; it is Buttercup, and now I must tell my friends what you have done so kindly."

I was sitting next to the golden doorway which was about the size of my thumbnail. I looked at the view over to Wales and breathed in the December air. "What a thing to do on Christmas day," I said to myself.

Then all of a sudden I heard lots of different excitable voices:

"Hooray!"

"Yippee!"

"Our door is back!"

"Oh, thank you!"

"Let's bring in the berries!"

Then, in front of my eyes, the fairies took them from the grass up in the air and to the little golden door. I had emptied the rucksack and the holly berries formed a neat pile in the middle of the rockery. Although all I could see were red berries floating in the air, I knew it was the fairies carrying them. Next, I heard a little voice:

"My name is Primrose. Buttercup said your dog knocked over a china plate today. We wondered if we could have a piece to commemorate this happy day?"

"Yes, of course you can," I replied. I went inside and looked in the bin. The bits of china were wrapped in newspaper. As I began to unwrap the newspaper, I saw something out of the window. I was startled, and shouted to Mum, "Look, there's confetti in the air!"

She walked into the kitchen and stood by me.

"It's alright Mimi, I've seen this before, they are only baby butterflies."

She went back to the sitting room to eat some Christmas pudding. I had an idea to take some pudding out to the fairies. I found the best bit of china and took it with the Christmas pudding to the little golden door and watched the fairies move both inside. Then I heard Buttercup:

"It was us dancing with blossom you thought was confetti in the air! We wanted to show our happiness to you, so we wrapped petals around us and danced outside of the window!"

"Oh!" I said. "So you were not butterflies after all!"

"No," said Buttercup. "In the spring we gather together blossom which has fallen from the trees and we wear it when it is very cold weather, and we use blossom petals for sheets too. Happy Christmas Mimi, from all of us!"

"Happy Christmas fairies!" I said.

"Who are you talking to?"

It was Gregor from next door. He was wearing a red hat with a fluffy white pom-pom at the end of it.

"The fairies," I said.

"Fairies? I didn't know we had fairies in England, Mimi! I thought they only lived in hot countries. If you are sure then prove it to me!"

"Okay, I will."

I ran indoors and got the magnifying glass and took it outside. I called out: "Buttercup, Primrose, where are you?" We stood together by the shrub at the end of the rockery.

"I think you are making this up, Mimi."

I replied to him that I wasn't, and then said: "I can hear them talk, but you won't be able to because you haven't eaten a special fruit." I continued, "When I was with my Aunt Florence, I ate a poisonous berry which I thought was a wild strawberry. Anyway, whatever it was I can now hear the fairies and they sometime wear blossom so I can see them too. Here's the magnifying glass, so when one talks to me she will probably be on my hand, and you can have a look."

"Okay," he said, "but what if I am standing on one now?"

"You probably are not because they see you coming and get out of the way." Then I heard Primrose speak:

"Mimi, I am down here!"

"Where?"

"I am sitting on an old snail's shell."

I looked down at my feet and saw a snail's shell.

"Let me see at once," Gregor said, "where do I look?"

I gave him the magnifying glass and pointed at the snail's shell. He bent down and peered at it. He saw a tiny fragile creature with what looked like leaf skeletons for wings. Then he said to me: "Wow, I'd never had believed you in a hundred years, but I do now!"

He stared at her and then another one appeared and I could just see that it was Buttercup. "Tell the boy that in the summer we go to his garden to sit under the daisies because more grow there than do here in your garden. When it's sunny we sit in the shade talking together in groups."

When I told him what Buttercup had said, he looked quite guilty, and said: "You and me, well, I mean, when you and I made daisy chains for our mums, we must have taken the sun parasols away from the fairies!"

"Oh, I'm sure they didn't mind," I said.

"The reason we group together is to talk to the daisy because we know the daisy has special yellow 'dust' which creates new fairies."

"Really?" I asked Primrose.

She went on, "We are here today because of the daisy petals and pollen which make us. If we group together and talk loud enough, the daisy may decide to make another fairy. It doesn't happen very often, but when it does we welcome a new fairy to the kingdom and give her a name that no other fairy has. The next new fairy when she eventually comes, we are going to call Honeysuckle."

"How do you know what to do?" I asked.

"Two of the older fairies, Chive and Clover, point out the daisies they think we should sit under. If we are sitting under a daisy and three petals fall, then we have to take them inside along with some yellow pollen, and then mix with fairy dust. We have a special bed inside and we put the white petals and pollen onto the blossom sheets. We wait overnight and then the next morning there is a new fairy."

I told Gregor everything she said, and he was fascinated. He looked at Primrose through the magnifying glass and asked her how long it had been since a new fairy had been made. She said it had been nine fairy years ago, and I worked this out to be late last spring. "There are no daisies around until February and only rare daisies listen. Buttercup is very good at talking under the daisies chosen by the older fairies to be the petal-dropping type. We talk loudly in a group about fairy life. Chive and Clover are the two oldest fairies so they have learnt from their experiences how to find a daisy which will listen. Occasionally the daisy they choose only sheds two petals; two of them is no good, it has to be three."

Suddenly there was a loud high-pitched sound. Gregor and I ran to the front of the house and saw Brian in his car. The car wasn't running and he kept hooting his horn. Flufftuff started barking franticly and stood up on his hind legs while stretching out his front paws. Then he started to scratch the wheels of the car. Brian saw us watching and said, "I've just mended the horn because it wasn't working properly, now it's as good as new. Now, what's my dog up to?"

Brian rolled his eyes up to the sky as Flufftuff started pawing the front tyre. A robin flew down from a branch onto the bonnet of the car. I knew a fairy was present.

"Hello Mimi, it's Buttercup. Our friendly robin has alerted us that a wheel is dangerously bald and Flufftuff picked up on it too. The robin had to tell me so I could tell you so you can tell Brian."

The robin had a twig of holly in its beak which fell out when he started to sing. I picked off the berries and put them in my pocket. Brian looked at me curiously and said, "Whenever I see you, you are either in Wellingtons back from the woods having collected holly or you are standing on the rockery with handfuls of berries! What are you up to

I wonder? Anyway, I shall be driving home tomorrow but I'd like to know you are alright before I set off."

"Oh, I'm perfectly fine," I told him. "It's you, Brian, I am worried about. The fairies have pointed out something to me, and I must tell you."

"Fairies?"

"Yes, the ones I told you about. There really are fairies living around here, and they have noticed your bald tyre. You might have an accident if you don't replace it."

Then I felt a tickle on my nose, and this time it was Chive who was sitting there, who said: "I am a very old fairy but to be young again I need to move away from here. I'd like to go with Brian and Flufftuff in the car tomorrow, to their garden."

I looked at Brian who was now taking a spare tyre out of the boot and preparing to replace the old one.

"That's good Brian, you will be safe now," I said. "There's a fairy sat on my nose now, Brian; she's called Chive."

"How long do they live for?" he asked.

"Actually," I said, "most fairies live forever, but if they fly into a holly leaf the spike can kill a fairy. It is the listening daisies that are responsible for making new fairies. An old fairy has been talking to me about moving on, so when she's somewhere new she can become young again."

"Oh," he said, "I never thought I'd hear myself say it, but if I was to believe in anything, then it would be fairies. However, there are stories about certain things like pixies, gnomes, gremlins and ghosts which I think are made up. Tell me more, Mimi."

"Well Brian, Chive wishes to go home with you and Flufftuff. I can line a matchbox with blossom so she can lie down during the journey. She will have loads of room but that doesn't matter as long as you keep the matchbox steady so it doesn't move about. She is forty-two fairy years old now but when she comes back in the spring she will be forty-one. The journey there and back turns the tide of age: instead of getting older her age will begin to descend. She will be forty next fairy year, then thirty-nine the next, then thirty-eight the next."

Chapter Four

GREGOR WENT HOME as it was getting late but I decided to show Brian the golden door to the kingdom before it got dark.

"Goodness gracious me!" he exclaimed.

I noticed his big walking boots and said, "Careful you don't kneel on Primrose or Buttercup because they are nearby."

"An actual tiny golden fairy door!" he said. "Well I never!"

Then, the door opened and I heard sounds, a bit like a choir singing but very quiet. I knew Brian couldn't hear, but for me it was spellbinding. Next, a moving thing appeared, and I saw it was a woodlouse with a little piece of soft material on its back. A fairy said, "We are celebrating today because our door is back! There are fifteen of us having a ride on Woody's back." Then I heard Mum's voice: "Time to come in Mimi and have some supper; you too, Brian, I've made some delicious quiche."

I found it difficult to tear myself away from the fairy door and was about to go when four more woodlice appeared one after another! Brian obviously couldn't hear them at all but could just see them.

"Why are they on woodlice if they have wings and can fly?" he asked.

"I think they just like to do something different occasionally," I replied, then added, "Let's go inside now and after supper I am going to find a matchbox for Chive to lie in while you drive home."

The next morning everybody was up and dressed early. All the fairies danced around the rockery and they wore pink blossom. Only Chive had a deep purple dress and I could just about see her tiny body too. Buttercup spoke: "By the time Chive comes back it should be spring, and spring means the flowers start to grow including daisies which means a new fairy will join us."

"Of course," I said to Buttercup, "I remember now, you are going to call her Honeysuckle."

She smiled and then said, "She can help us take care of Thyme. This herb has been quite dull recently. We have been flying around it trying to help it get more nutrition from the soil. That's what fairies do; if a plant is in poor condition, we do our best to make it feel better. We put fairy dust into the ground so that it reaches the plant roots and this is really good for mending any damage."

Then I understood why our plants and flowers always

looked much healthier and livelier than other people's gardens do. We have the magic that comes from the fairy kingdom beneath the rockery, which they don't.

Primrose and Buttercup were in the kingdom, collecting holly berry juice for Chive to take on the journey. As I bent down to look for them, the golden door opened and two primrose petals flew out in front of me. I took the magnifying glass out of my pocket and looked through it. Buttercup and Primrose looked very dainty in their splendid flower dresses. I could see their frail wings flapping fast. 'Dandelion seeds' is the best way to describe the wings— almost transparent and easily blown around in the wind. I had read at Aunt Florence's that when the spring comes and seeds are airborne, that the fairies love to fly all around them, between them, and above and under them. If a fairy makes a wish to ride on a dandelion seed because her wings are feeling weak, then often her wish is granted. All she must do is fly up the stem to the seeds and sit down on one of them and wait for the wind to blow her into the air.

Chive was sitting on the windscreen wiper of Brian's car, Primrose said. "She's quite nervous about leaving the kingdom until spring, but I keep telling her that it's not that long away really."

"Well," I said, "I have got the matchbox ready for her."

I walked to the car and carefully put the box on the bonnet. Chive stepped in and looked around and settled down. An hour later Brian and Flufftuff were outside, both having eaten a hearty breakfast. Mum and Dad said their goodbyes and said how wonderful Christmas had been. When he'd put Flufftuff on his rug on the back seat, he got into the driving seat. He wound the window down so I could talk to him. "Chive is in this little matchbox all set up and ready for the journey," I said. "You must not let the box fall around while you are travelling because it could damage her wings, and also, the holly berry juice must be kept upright. To check halfway that she is alright, have a look at her through the magnifying glass."

I gave him the box and the magnifying glass, and we exchanged kisses.

"What do I do with her when I get home?"

"Well Brian, she must be introduced to the fairy community in your garden, which you never knew of before, and then say goodbye to her."

Next I heard the other older fairy, Clover, talk: "I am forty-two fairy years old too, and 1 am worried to be apart from my best friend for so long."

I could see her hovering in front of me in her tiny pink petal dress. Then I was struck with an idea, and this was for Clover to go along with Chive in Brian's car.

"How about going too?" I said.

"I can't because I am scared of travelling in a car," she said.

"Don't be scared," I heard Chive say. "If you don't come with us," she said to Clover, "then when I return I will get younger and younger, and you will continue to get even older. How will we remain so close if we have so much age between us?"

"Age doesn't matter to me," said Clover, adding, "it doesn't change a thing, and we will always be best friends."

"It's time to go!" said Brian. He wound up the window, waved goodbye and started up the engine. Flufftuff poked his head out of the back window and barked to say "cheerio". Mum, Dad and I stood at the porch, Mum waving her hanky and Dad waving his wallet. I breathed a big sigh when the car disappeared from sight.

"That's a heavy sigh Mimi, are you going to miss Brian and Flufftuff?"

"Yes Mum, it's quite a long time until we see them again."

"It will be spring before you know it, it's only three months away."

"Will Brian phone when he gets home, Mum?"

"Yes, and you can speak to him later when he does."

At least then I'd know that Chive was safe. Also I needed to tell Brian where in his garden I thought was best to open the matchbox. I remembered he had a pond with stones around it, and I thought the fairies might live there. I would tell him what to do when he phoned.

It was still winter and I wondered how the fairies manage to keep warm in the cold, often bitterly cold weather.

"We cope alright Mimi," said Clover to me one morning. "We don't feel the cold because we are not warm blooded like you are, or mammals are. We don't have blood at all you know; we are magical like that. Each one of us is important to each other no matter how old we may be. A fairy can't feel cold but can feel lonely if she has no friends. My closest friend is Chive and I know I have to wait quite a few years until we are united again. It is not years to you Mimi, to you it is only three months until April, but to me it is three and a half fairy years to see Chive again."

Chapter Five

IT WAS SOON sunny again with all the daffodils and bluebells coming out. I hadn't been very involved with the fairies during January and February because the cold wet weather did not entice me to go in the garden much. Now it was the end of March and the weather was a lot nicer, and I was enjoying sitting in a deck chair absorbing the sun. I had homework to do which was okay, as I liked school these days. I never used to, but now in art class I was loving painting huge fairies, trying to think where they would all live if they were as big as me.

One day Clover pointed out a particular daisy in Gregor's garden for the younger fairies to sit under. She told me that the daisy she picked out should be a likely one to make a new fairy. I wanted to see for myself so I went through the hole in the hedge which separated my garden from Gregor's. There were loads of daisies scattered all over the lawn. I went to the back door and knocked. Gregor's mum opened the kitchen window and said, "Hi Mimi, what's up?"

"I just wondered if I could sit in the sun in your garden?"

"Well, that won't be much fun on your own."

"I don't mind."

"Gregor is in his bedroom, I'll give him a call and let him know you are here."

While I waited for him, Clover spoke again: "This tall daisy by the rose tree is the one, Mimi."

I walked over to the tree and saw a small collection of daisies. The tall one she had chosen was the tallest one there and the one in the middle.

"I'm going to get some younger fairies now," she said. "We have nominated ten to do the honour. In the build-up to spring all of us have taken great care in all that we do. We have to have the most careful and deserving fairies to sit under the daisy. Right! I'm going to get them, cheerio."

I stared at the daisy she had pointed out to me. It looked extremely healthy compared to the others.

"Hi Mimi!" It was Gregor walking towards me. He was wearing a flashy pair of trainers and blue shorts and with it a chequered short-sleeved T-shirt. He looked very summery, I thought. "Remember how you told me a new fairy is made?"

"Yeah?"

"I'm going to try to make one myself!"

"You can't do that!"

"Why not Mimi? There's no law saying I can't."

Suddenly I saw him in a different light. With his stupid trainers and his summer get up, he was meddling with fairy magic.

"What have you done?" I asked him.

He came up closer to me and said, "I picked a daisy yesterday and pulled it apart!"

I was horrified.

"Then," he continued, "I put the petals with some of the yellow pollen into an old ring box, and that's it, really."

"It won't work, Gregor. The petals have to fall naturally to the ground; not picked off like you have done."

We went upstairs and into Gregor's bedroom. He had football posters on the walls and prints of footballs on his duvet.

"Is this the box?" I asked. I had been drawn to the window sill where a small box sat, next to a dinky toy car.

"Yes Mimi." He opened the box and we saw a whole daisy complete with all its petals, a middle and a stem.

I gasped and said, "So all you did was pick a daisy and put it in this box?"

"Yeah, I was joking about taking petals off and trying to make a new fairy."

"Are you sure you haven't tried before?" (I knew him inside out and suspected he had tried before and his efforts had failed.)

"I'm back!" It was Clover's voice. "The ten chosen

fairies have flown here with me and now I shall show them the daisy which should make a new fairy."

The ten chosen fairies were wearing blossom dresses, and luckily for me and Gregor, we could see them, just. They danced in circles and then positioned themselves under the daisy. I thought to myself that a daisy to fairies must be very tall, reaching up to the sky. Then all of a sudden I heard them chatting to each other. They talked about the kingdom, about the plants they help when they are sick, and about what they know of human beings.

Gregor asked, "Can I go and check the little box with the petals and pollen in it?"

"I still believe it is wrong to do what you've done," I said.

"Come in with me," he said, "and have a look through *my* magnifying glass."

"Well, actually, I have," I said.

"Last weekend," he said, "I picked off three petals and put them in the box with the yellow pollen, but when I checked, nothing happened overnight."

"I'm not surprised," I said. I was annoyed at him for doing this. We both said nothing more, standing looking out of the window.

Chapter Six

THAT EVENING I went home feeling very excited. Tomorrow I would find out if the chosen daisy had listened to the chosen fairies underneath it. The question was, would three petals fall? I found it difficult to sleep, so started counting sheep in my head. I was still awake at twelve o'clock thinking about Honeysuckle's arrival.

I woke up to the sound of rain pattering on the window. I went downstairs to find Dad cooking bacon and eggs.

"Morning Mimi. It's about time I treated you to a yummy cooked breakfast."

"Um, thanks Dad, but first I have to go outside to see if…"

He looked at me with a look that said he wasn't in the mood for fairy talk.

"To see if?"

"Oh no Dad, it's nothing."

I sat down at the table and fiddled with the pepper mill. The fairies would be in the kingdom now, I thought to myself, and if it didn't stop raining, then I wouldn't be able to find out about the new expected one. The rain continued to pour down.

"Hi Mimi, it's Buttercup. I flew under the back door and now I am on the pepper mill!"

Dad had his back to me so I whispered to her: "Buttercup, stay where you are, then after breakfast we can go upstairs to my bedroom."

"Okay," she said, "I know that if you start talking to me now then he will think you are being silly again."

I sat patiently until the bacon and eggs were cooked and it was put on the table. I ate quickly and then got up from the table and went upstairs. I said aloud, "Buttercup, did you get soaked in the rain?"

"Well actually, when I left the kingdom at 6 a.m. it wasn't raining, so I flew over here in case you were up early. I wanted to tell you the sad news which is that three petals did not fall from the listening daisy yesterday. I have been waiting here on the pepper mill wondering, as has everybody else, why the petals did not fall. If the rain eases off, we are going to sit under another daisy today and try again."

"I'm so sorry nothing happened, Buttercup. I know all the fairies thought Clover had chosen the most likely daisy. Could it be that she is missing her friend Chive so much that her judgement has been altered?"

"That could be it, she does think a lot about Chive. When will she be back?"

"Very soon," I said.

The rain did not stop all day. I sat inside watching TV with Lucky our cat to keep me company. Mum and Dad had gone out to some sort of meeting. Lucky began washing behind her ears and licking her front paws to clean herself. She was jet black apart from a white patch on her tummy. We had had her since she was a kitten and now she was fully grown and always contented.

The next-day was sunny again. Clover had chosen another daisy in Gregor's garden, and today the ten young fairies were chatting excitedly under it.

Later, when I got home from school I went outside and waited by the little fairy golden door. In a minute or two I heard Primrose's voice:

"While you were at school, we brought inside three petals and yellow fairy pollen. Tomorrow we will have a brand new fairy! It's so exciting, Mimi."

I smiled a huge smile at the news and went to bed that night early so I'd be up early too. When I awoke I saw a primrose petal hovering near my window. It was Primrose again, dancing merrily.

"Honeysuckle has arrived, Mimi! She is in the kingdom at the moment getting introduced to everyone. Her wings are perfect and her voice sounds great. She has drunk some holly berry juice which she said tasted fantastic."

This is great news, I thought to myself, but I sensed something was wrong so I said, "Is everything else alright?"

"Well actually," said Primrose, "no."

"Why, what's wrong?"

She hesitated and then told me that yesterday a vole had scratched at some soil, manoeuvred a stone and poked its nose into the kingdom.

"We need someone to protect the kingdom from these nosey rodents."

"What about Lucky?"

"Yes, Lucky loves chasing small animals."

I thought about this idea more and more, and it seemed the perfect solution.

Then Primrose said: "As she sleeps we will sprinkle fairy dust on her back so when she wakes up she will know she is the guardian of the fairy kingdom."

"That's a good idea," I said.

"As Honeysuckle is our brand new fairy, we shall ask her to do this, but now Mimi, I should return to the kingdom to see her."

I followed Primrose outside and went up the rockery to see the golden door open for her. When it closed behind her, I sat down on a flat rock and stared at the view. I thought back to when I was amongst those hills in Wales, in Aunt Florence's house. Her fairy books had not been about how fairies were made, (I'd found that out myself) but did tell of the fairy dust with all its different uses. Cats are particularly sensitive to the fairy dust and they will help guard the fairies by pouncing on any intruder like the vole or the rat.

Lucky's black coat would turn yellow when sprinkled with fairy dust. What would Mum and Dad think? Next, I heard Mum calling me, telling me that Brian was on the phone. I went inside and as I went to the phone I noticed Lucky curled up on the armchair. I thought again about cats and fairies in Aunt Florence's books. If cats are able to guard fairies, then can they see them properly or only a little, like I can? I held on to this thought; saved it for later when I could think about it more.

Brian spoke: "I am bringing your fairy back to you this weekend. Every time I look at her, which is just in the evening, she always points at a wavy leaf!"

"Why?" I asked.

"I really don't know, Mimi. She has put this leaf, (with some help I presume) into the matchbox and I think she would like to bring it home."

"That's okay, I will ask her what it's for when you come back."

"Alright then, today is Wednesday and we shall start our journey to you on Friday afternoon."

"See you then Brian, bye."

"Bye, Mimi."

Chapter Seven

THE NEXT DAY Primrose and Buttercup were together, flying near me as I sat outside in a deckchair.

"Hi, Mimi!"

I wasn't sure which one was talking. "One moment, let me get the magnifying glass," I said.

I ran into the lounge and found it in the drawer where it was always kept. Looking at them both together, I could see that their bodies were exactly the same sizes but that Buttercup's wings were slightly bigger than Primrose's.

"As I said before, sweet girl of the rockery," (it was Buttercup talking) "one of the things for Honeysuckle to do is to look after the herb thyme. Remember how I told you we need a brand new fairy for this job?"

"Yes," I said, "I remember you saying that you all look after sickly plants. We have no honeysuckle in the garden, but if we did, would Honeysuckle look after the honeysuckle?"

"I don't know who would look after this majestic plant. It is in fact a fairy favourite. It is a shame we have none in the garden or in any nearby gardens." Buttercup continued talking to me while balancing on my nose.

"Where is the cat?" she asked.

"Asleep under the hedge over there."

"Perfect! I shall go and get Honeysuckle and we shall put magic dust on her."

She flew off, leaving Primrose and me to stare at Lucky. I was curious about where the magic dust came from.

"Well," said Primrose, smoothing down her wings and sitting down, "I don't know where it originally came from but what I do know is that we have an endless supply, and that it has been with us for hundreds of generations."

"Oh I see."

After five minutes Buttercup returned with Honeysuckle and between them they carried a jar of glittering magic dust.

"Don't be afraid of the cat," I heard Primrose tell Honeysuckle. "Cats do not dig into our kingdom because they know that a rockery is a special place. When we put magic dust onto Lucky, she will fully understand that she is needed by all the fairies as a guardian."

I watched as all three fairies flew over the cat's back and sprinkled magic dust in a swirly line on her black coat of fur. She didn't wake up, she just sighed and put a paw over her face, as if to hide. When she did wake up, she went all over the rockery, treading carefully and taking it all in. Some other fairies followed her around and when she paused and looked up they flew in front of her, dancing from side to side.

She caught two voles that day, and from that day on she never forgot her duty to the kingdom. I thought to myself that without the magic dust, she would be just a normal cat who sleeps and eats all day. Now she is Lucky the Fairy Guardian, fearless of intruders and protector of all fairies. Her coat did turn yellow just on her back. It looked like someone had spilt paint over her. She didn't seem to mind though and continued treading (with caution) around the rockery. I thought to myself that perhaps I should tell the truth about how Lucky had acquired a yellow stripe on her coat. Mum and Dad were bound to ask me if I knew anything about it.

Chapter Eight

I REMEMBERED one bit in Aunt Florence's books explaining that grown-ups probably would be unable to see fairies even if they looked through a magnifying glass. It said that fairies didn't want grown-ups to know about them. How can I explain about Lucky's coat, I wondered? Then I heard Mum say to Dad:

"The cat is acting strange and I think Mimi has dyed his coat too!"

Now I was in trouble. "Mum, that yellow is magic fairy dust and I watched it being sprinkled on."

"I don't believe you Mimi, what really happened?"

Well, if she wouldn't accept the truth, then a made-up story was the best I could do. I remembered my watercolours upstairs in my drawer and said:

"Okay, well, Lucky was watching me paint; I was using the yellow paint and when I washed my brush she knocked over the jar of water which mixed with the yellow paint. Then she slipped over on my picture, causing a big mess and putting yellow on her coat."

"Well, let's hope it washes off in the rain," she said.

I thought Lucky looked striking with the yellow stripe she now had. To find if the colour would wash off or not, I decided to get a wet sponge and see. It did not wash off which hardly surprised me because it was magic dust that had been poured on her back, not paint.

After school the next day I sat outside the house, ready to greet Brian and Flufftuff. They arrived at seven o' clock and by this time I had become quite tired. I noticed Brian step out of the car carefully, holding the matchbox with a steady hand. I took it from him and gave him a hug and a kiss. I went up to my bedroom, sat on my bed and opened the matchbox. I saw Chive stand up and point out to me the wavy leaf she had, folded, with her.

"Hi Mimi!" she said. "I am so grateful to Brian taking me to his home and back. I am a younger fairy now; I'm so happy!"

"Clover has missed you terribly," I said, in a concerned voice. She nodded, then flew into the air and told me she had a great secret to tell:

"I have to tell you something but first I must say 'hello' to Clover."

Later when I was sitting on the rockery on a flat bit of stone, Chive told me and all the other fairies about her secret—a secret called 'Forget-me-not'. Chive had asked me to carry the matchbox outside.

"Look what's inside," she said. "This is not a leaf, it is a fairy!"

The fairies in their blossom dresses flew over the box to get a good look in.

"The fairies in Brian's garden are much bigger than us. They can use magic dust to make themselves look like leaves!"

Buttercup responded: "So this leaf is called 'Forget-me-not' and is really a fairy then?"

"Yes, watch her stand up!" said Chive.

The folded fairy stood up, and in a blink of the eye, was no longer looking like a leaf. She was as big as my hand. All the rockery fairies were astonished. Forget-me-not gracefully spread her wings which were purple, matching the colour of her magical stunning dress. She was amazing and left me speechless.

Lucky entered during all this excitement and jumped up on the bed. She saw Forget-me-not but then looked at me and started meowing. Forget-me-not looked at her and asked, "Is this cat the guardian of the kingdom here?"

"Yes," said Honeysuckle, "she knows what to do if any nosy voles start to dig into the kingdom. We have only just made her our guardian; the yellow stripe shows she has fairy dust sprinkled on her back."

"Oh how lovely!" remarked Forget-me-not who then asked if she could look around the kingdom, if she would fit. Only Chive had given this situation a moment of thought and said, "It was easy for me to go into the kingdom of the large leaf fairies at Brian's, but it would be impossible for Forget-me-not to be a guest in our tiny home. She can spend all day in the garden amongst the plants and shrubs, but when evening comes I think she should stay with you, Mimi."

I nodded, still amazed at what was before me. I smiled at Forget-me-not, and she spoke again: "It's alright, I don't need to go inside to see that part of the kingdom. I can appreciate the rockery and its magic outside, but I will not let any adult see me though. If an adult comes near me, then I will change to look like a leaf until they have gone."

I decided that I'd make a soft bed in a shoe box for the fairy.

As the days passed, she felt more and more at home in my bedroom. If I was writing or painting, she would sit on my desk next to me and when I was watching TV she'd sit near me where my soft teddies were. She'd sit back between Ted's arms and often fall asleep there rather in the bed I had made for her.

One evening I told her all about the way fairies were made, from three petals of a daisy. She said that Chive had tried to explain but that it was easier coming from me for her to understand.

"This is the first time ever that we have known about each other."

I knew what Forget-me-not meant, which was that the tiny fairies did not know until now that the larger leaf fairies existed and vice-versa. She told me that in Brian's garden there was a deciduous tree by the pond. The branches spread high above the water, and in the autumn the leaves which were golden brown fell into it and floated on top.

"This is how we are made," she said. "Each leaf landing on the pond becomes a 'leaf fairy' and will live forever. My friend Lavender and I were two leaves which fell together into the water, and we were the first to notice Chive. Brian drove up to the house and put the matchbox next to the pond. The dog sniffed at it and then lost interest and went inside."

"Oh, Flufftuff is always trying to find things out," I said, "he is quite boisterous and I suppose that you keep well out of his way!"

"Yes we do, Mimi. Anyway, Lavender and I were curious to see what was so special that it had to be placed in a little box. When Brian had gone in, we cautiously went over to where he'd placed it and looked in. We had a quick glimpse of tiny Chive, who flew away with fright."

"To her you must seem like giants!"

"Yes, we would appear huge to Chive, just as people appear huge to us, the leaf fairies."

"What happened next?" I asked.

"Well, we spotted her by the pebbles arranged for show at the lower end of the garden. (Brian had brought the pebbles back from the beach one day.) We went over to her and told her not to be scared; she had been watching us."

"I expect her little heart had been beating fast."

"Yes, by now she had realised we were fairies too and

that it was silly to be frightened of us. She smiled at us and said she needed shelter because she was staying until spring."

Just then, Lucky came into the bedroom, meowing at us and seeming troubled. She had three fairies flying near her head.

"Mimi?"

"Yes?" I said.

"It's me, Buttercup, and Primrose and Honeysuckle too."

"Whatever is the matter?"

Primrose spoke: "Lucky has been guarding the kingdom so well. There was the same rabbit in the garden today who blocked up the doorway with his droppings before. Lucky caught him doing this again and chased him away. Poor Lucky—we think she has been stung on her nose by a wasp."

Forget-me-not flew onto Lucky's back and said that she could heal her. She sprinkled fairy dust on her face, and especially her nose. She stopped meowing and licked her nose several times. Her eyes shut and she started to purr.

"Mimi, you are still my best friend," said Buttercup. "Wasp stings can be fatal to cats and we don't have the healing fairy dust to stop the pain. Without Forget-me-not's superior fairy dust, Lucky would have had to go to the vet."

I watched Lucky curl up on the bed quite better now, and stroked her until she went to sleep. I noticed she'd been molting because the weather had been hot. There were clumps of fur on the chair she usually sat on.

Chapter Nine

I **WENT DOWNSTAIRS** to talk to Dad. "So you say these fairies live in the moss in the garden?" he asked. I decided I wanted Dad to really know about them.

"Yes Dad," I replied, "hundreds of fairies live on the rockery."

He looked like he wanted me to show him, so I said: "Right then, follow me and see for yourself." (I didn't think the fairies would mind if just one adult knew of them, especially as this was only my dad.)

We went into the garden with the magnifying glass and stopped by a big stone covered in moss. We waited for an hour—the fairies were a bit shy. Eventually Buttercup, Primrose, Chive and Clover turned up.

"Look Dad!"

He gasped when he looked through the magnifying glass and saw all four fairies dancing in a circle.

"I don't believe my eyes, Mimi! You have kept this a secret for a long time!"

"I haven't, actually—I told you all about them last Christmas."

"I can't remember, did you?"

"Yes Dad. I told you that they live behind the rockery in the garden and how they take care of any sick plants that need their care."

"Wow!" Dad said, "They are so tiny! What do they eat?"

"As I told you before, they survive on holly berries."

"Holly berries? Hmmmm, oh yes, *now* I remember. Last Christmas you took all the red berries off the holly we had in the house, didn't you? You also went into the woods to get more."

"Yes Dad, they called me 'sweet girl of the rockery' and asked me if I would do this favour for them."

"The world should know about this!" he said.

In a very short time all the neighbours were queuing up to see the marvel. Dad told everyone he knew and people came from all over to our garden to see if what he claimed to be true really was. The trouble was no one believed him. I knew the fairies were not prepared to let other people see them. Neighbours visited and waited and waited but did not see anything.

When the people had all gone, I went to the golden door and called out: "Hey fairies, it's safe to come out now!" They had all been inside the kingdom for days. Dad felt quite special because he had been able to see four fairies, but no-one else apart from me or Gregor could.

That evening the fairies were on the rockery flying between shrubs and herbs. It was late, nearly ten o'clock so I went upstairs to bed. As I tried to sleep I heard an owl outside. The hooting sound kept me awake. I looked out of my window and saw a bright half-moon. The garden was lit up in the moonlight. Forget-me-not was fast asleep in Ted's arms.

Then I heard Honeysuckle: "Come outside, sweet girl of the rockery, we are making the most of the warm summer night."

I put my dressing gown and slippers on and, careful not to wake Forget-me-not, I left the bedroom. I crept quietly downstairs and past the sitting room where Mum and Dad were still watching television. I went through to the kitchen to the back door which I unlocked and closed behind myself as quietly as possible. There were hundreds of fairies flying around wearing different dresses. Some were blossom petals, some primrose petals and some were even wearing rose petals.

"We are all out tonight because the owl is hooting," said Buttercup, continuing: "The owl knows about us and it is always nice to sit up in the branches with him. His wife is sitting on three eggs which might hatch very soon, which would make tonight a very special occasion."

I looked up at the branches and spotted the barn owls together. The female owl was sitting on her eggs in the hollow of the tree, while the male was perched on a nearby branch.

"I love owls," I said aloud. They looked at me, then blinked and then smoothed down their feathers. I sat down on the grass and watched the fairies fly around the two owls, spreading their magic dust. There was some plywood by the trunk of the tree which Dad had left. The tiny fairies sprinkled fairy dust everywhere, even on the plywood. As I watched, the wood began to shimmer a gold and silver colour. The owls seemed to notice and began hooting even more.

"Is there a reason you put magic dust on the plywood?" I asked Primrose.

"Yes Mimi. As your Dad knows we are here now, he could make us a holiday home out of plywood."

"Why do you need a holiday home?" I asked.

"Well, we want to go to Forget-me-not's home at Brian's to meet the other Leaf Fairies."

"Oh I see."

Just then the rosemary by the base of the tree moved as if something had landed in it. All at once the fairies darted to the shrub. They hovered over it looking down at it in their pink dresses. They formed a pink cloud over the top of the rosemary plant. I had a look for myself and saw that one of the owl's eggs had fallen from the nest. Luckily the rosemary plant had broken the fall, and given a soft landing. The fairies tried to lift the egg but with no success. I looked up at the owls who had stopped hooting and who looked at me with pleading eyes, so I picked up the egg.

"I'll carry it, Mimi!" It was Forget-me-not; she had flown out of the window and was now sitting on my knee.

"Won't it be too heavy for you?" I asked.

"No," she said, "I can support it in my skirt, and I haven't got far to go, if you reach up as far as you can."

I held the eggs as high as possible, and Forget-me-not took it from my hand and carried it up to the owls. She then put it into the nest next to the other two eggs. She flew back to me and rested in my hand.

I then heard Dad calling me: "Come in please, it's late and it's dark. This is no time for playing with fairies."

He walked towards me, and suddenly Forget-me-not looked startled. He had a few steps to go, and then he might see her. I looked at my hand and saw a green leaf as she had transformed herself just in time. I put her down on the grass and went inside.

When I got to my bedroom Forget-me-not had flown through the window and had changed back into her fairy self.

"Those owls were really pleased to get their eggs back," said Forget-me-not.

"Yes," I said, "if you hadn't been there to carry it, then I suppose all the tiny fairies would have managed to carry it somehow."

"Buttercup and everyone else are still up in the tree, waiting to see if the eggs hatch."

I went to draw the curtains so I could see the garden still in the moonlight.

"Oh well, Forget-me-not," I said, "let's try and get some sleep." I snuggled up under the duvet and shut my eyes.

The owls kept hooting; it was now midnight and I was *still* awake. I could hear a noise every now and again, like someone was opening and closing something. I peered out of the window again and saw Lucky race across the lawn. She darted around and then went to the back door. I heard the noise again and realised it was the cat flap closing shut every time she went in and out. I went back to bed but kept tossing and turning, trying to sleep on my right side, then the left. Eventually I put the light on and looked at the clock. It was 2.30 a.m. I tried reading for a while but still didn't feel sleepy. The cat flap went again and in a minute or two, Lucky pushed the door open and jumped on the bed. Another hour passed and then I went to sleep.

Chapter Ten

THE NEXT MORNING was a Saturday. I awoke at 11 a.m. to see the sunshine streaming through the window. Lucky had long gone but there were tufts of fur left on the bed where she had been lying during the night. I went downstairs to get some cereal for Forget-me-not, and I saw Mum was cooking bacon and eggs.

"Why do you take your breakfast to your bedroom, Mimi?"

"Oh, no reason really Mum, I just like to."

I was chuffed that Mum didn't really mind me doing this and that she didn't ask any more questions. I took the cereal up to Forget-me-not, who leaned over the edge of the bowl to eat cornflakes one by one. She didn't have a big appetite and only ate three flakes. She scooped up the milk by cupping her hands and drinking like that. She smiled at me and said, "You know, I *love* cornflakes. Leaf fairies have their own cereal—a mixture of weetabix, cornflakes and muesli."

I was very interested at this and urged her to tell me more. "Who gives you the food?" I asked.

Forget-me-not looked from side to side and behind which to me looked like she was going to tell a secret and didn't want to be overheard. "In the tree trunk of the tree from which we were mad, is all our food." She smiled again and continued: "The tree is so very special to us because without the food inside it we would all die."

Then, a thought came to me, and I asked Forget-me-not: "Is your fairy food tree the only one in the world or are there more?"

"Ours is the only one, we know that. There's a hole which takes you into the tree and at the bottom of the tree trunk there is a sparkly box. We can open the box when we want which we do quite often."

"What's in it?" I asked.

"Well, food of course," she said, "and a notepad with writing on it saying: *This is the only fairy food leaf tree in the world.*' Also, there is a bunch of freesias which are very pretty flowers."

I thought about it and then said, "I know they are extremely pretty; they are coloured from light pinks, dark pinks to purples and yellows, and they smell divine."

"Yes," said Forget-me-not. "These flowers, Mimi, are not ordinary flowers. Although in a dark box most of the time, they never wilt and don't need water. They are never-ending freesias; always fresh despite no sunlight. No Leaf fairy knows why they are there or what they are for."

"Let's try and find out," I said. Forget-me-not then went into great detail, saying how she and her friend Lavender believed that fairy dust could come from these very delicately perfumed flowers. She explained that at home in Brian's garden, the fairy dust used for healing sick plants was all different colours and sparkled in the dark. She said it was in a big pot kept in the tree trunk. Fairies could fly into the trunk and fill their little shoulder bags with magic dust. Then, Forget-me-not explained that the magic fairy dust had several uses. The main use I already knew of was to get sick plants well (the same as the tiny fairies) and make them happier in the soil. Also though, if sprinkled onto a small animal then it might change into a different animal. "A bit like a magic wand; the leaf fairies dust has great powers," she told me. "An example of this was when a fox was prowling in our garden, there was a rabbit running away from him, so to protect the rabbit, one of the leaf fairies turned the fox into another rabbit. So when the rabbit reached the other rabbit, they rubbed noses which was far better than one taking the other home for supper."

I agreed with her that it was far better that way. I thought to myself that although all very interesting, it still didn't solve the puzzle of why the freesias were in the leaf fairy food tree. Forget-me-not sighed and said, "No leaf fairy knows, but I think maybe Buttercup or Chive might know, *if* they were taken to see the flowers themselves."

"How would they know?" I asked.

"They just seem the cleverest of all the fairies in the kingdom here. I had a hole in my dress and Chive mended it for me so it looks just like new. And Buttercup, she told me how a journey to Brian's can reverse age so the older fairies come back younger. This all sounds very mathematical and complicated." She frowned and I could see she had become quite attached to these two fairies.

"I think Buttercup and Chive should definitely have a look," I said. "I'm going to ask Dad to make a fairy hotel from the plywood which had shimmered in the moonlight the night the owls' egg fell from the tree."

I went downstairs and found Dad with his feet up relaxing to some soft music. He had just washed the car inside and out, and before that he had been finding the best places to hang some pictures on the walls. I went over to him and said, "Dad, could you make something special for the fairies from that plywood in the garden?"

"How would I do that, Mimi?" he asked.

"Well Dad, all you have to do is make one side with lots of ledges like a spice rack and then I will line the inside with lots of green soft moss. That's all there is to it."

The next day Primrose told me which clumps of moss I could dig up. I took a trowel and while Dad was hammering and sawing the plywood, I carefully pulled up the moss. Many fairies were watching him as he constructed a home ideal for their use. Clover and Honeysuckle whispered in my ear how the home should mimic the inside of their kingdom. Honeysuckle explained how each fairy had its own little bed; the mattress was made from rabbit fur and the sheets were made from blossom petals. There were little tables and chairs made from crystal quartz behind the rockery specifically for the fairies, which made the kingdom.

Honeysuckle flew over to the part of the garden which had tiny stones in it. She said: "We can't move the quartz from inside the kingdom, so instead you could pick out the smoothest and tiniest stones here please, Mimi." I was happy to do this and while I was choosing the whitest ones which I thought were the prettiest I could hear Clover and Honeysuckle singing close by.

Dad had made a space in the hotel for the holly berry juice. We could only guess how much juice would be needed because no one knew how long they'd be away. We put the juice in two egg cups and put foil on top. Then I placed the egg cups in the space Dad had made especially for them.

"Is this alright?" Dad asked, pointing to the plywood hotel he had finished.

"Oh, it's perfect, let the fairies have a look inside!" I said.

Buttercup, Primrose and Chive flew into the hotel followed by Clover, Honeysuckle and many others. Then, I heard a voice I hadn't heard for a while:

"Hi Mimi, what are you doing?" It was Gregor. He still didn't know the news about Honeysuckle's arrival.

"Last week," I told him, "the three petals *did* fall from the second chosen daisy in your garden and a new fairy was made."

"Wow!" he said, "Let's see her! Where is she?"

"She is inside the plywood hotel choosing a bed for herself for when they go away."

"Go away, Mimi? Go away where?"

"To Brian's house where the leaf fairies live."

He looked at me quizzically, probably wondering what a leaf fairy was. I didn't have to explain though because Forget-me-not flew onto my shoulder. Gregor was both amazed and surprised:

"So, the Leaf Fairies are huge, like this one?"

"Yes," I replied as he stared at her. He stayed all afternoon, talking to Forget-me-not, who he could see, unlike the tiny fairies.

Honeysuckle heard that the boy from next door wanted to see her and said to Buttercup: "I shall sit on top of this stone near the rosemary plant in the middle of the rockery; then, if he looks hard enough he can see me."

I put a blade of grass on the stone to show where she was. He said, "Do I need the magnifying glass?" He was squinting at the blade of grass. He suddenly said aloud: "I see her! I see her!"—and as he looked, she did a pirouette.

Honeysuckle was still regarded as the 'newby' to the other fairies. She had yet to learn how to cast spells using the magic dust. The Fairy Queen had not taught her how to do this. I had seen the Fairy Queen before. She was a lot bigger than the others, though. Her wings were as large as the size of fully grown butterfly wings. She had a gold anklet on her right ankle and gold bangles on her wrists. Her hair was long and black and she wore a blue scarf around her waist and a blue headband too. She was about two inches tall and very elegant. She was usually behind the rockery telling stories to the other fairies, but she had come out before, especially to meet Forget-me-not.

Gregor looked a lot at Honeysuckle until she got irritated. She flew over to him and dropped a whole bag full of magic dust on him. The next thing I knew, Gregor was shouting, "Oh no, oh no, I've got a rabbit's tail!"

Sure enough, he had a rabbit's bobtail on his bottom! He tried to pull it off saying: "Ouch, it's really stuck! Your silly fairy has cast a spell on me. Please make her reverse it now Mimi."

I turned to Honeysuckle who was crying. "Don't be sad," I said and then went on: "Go and ask the Fairy Queen how to reverse the spell." She continued to cry—in fact, she was crying with laughter!

She went through the tiny golden door into the kingdom. In twenty minutes or so she came out again looking more composed. Then in a minute the Fairy Queen appeared too. She looked at Gregor's bobtail, and said: "This has never happened before and I don't know how to reverse the spell."

Gregor wailed, "You don't know! You *must* know, I can't go home like this!"

Then Buttercup spoke: "I have a suggestion. Mimi is the

sweet girl of the rockery and my best friend. Now, I think that if she were given some fairy dust in her own hand and then sprinkled it on Gregor's tail, and said something, then it might just be her good luck which could reverse the spell."

"Very good Buttercup," said the Fairy Queen, "Buttercup's ideas for some reason have always worked. Now I'm going inside to get the magic dust."

Gregor laid down on his front on the grass. The Fairy Queen came back and gave me the fairy magic dust. "You could try saying," she said to me, *"Vanish tail, vanish tail."* I did what I was told and amazingly the rabbit's tail disappeared from Gregor's bottom!

Forget-me-not had been watching all of this. "Your magic dust can do incredible things," she said to the Fairy Queen who had her arms around Honeysuckle.

The Fairy Queen looked up at the leaf fairy, and said: "Now Mimi's Dad has finished the plywood home, it won't be long until my fairies can see your kingdom which I've heard is inside a tree trunk, or something like that."

I looked at all three fairies: Honeysuckle who was so tiny I could hardly see, the Fairy Queen who was two inches tall, and like a porcelain fairy found in the shops, and lastly Forget-me-not who was the biggest of them all. Dad had told me earlier that day that he would be driving the tiny fairies to Brian's house tomorrow, so I told this to the Fairy Queen. She said: "Primrose and Buttercup will put some magic dust over the car's engine, just to make sure there will not be any breakdowns. Let's do this now; can you open the bonnet please Mimi?"

I went inside to get the car keys, brought them to the car and opened the bonnet. I watched the two fairies sprinkle gold and silver magic dust all over the engine. Some of the other fairies joined in and soon the cold engine was sparkling.

Forget-me-not was on my shoulder but soon changed into a leaf when Dad appeared.

"Have you packed a few things for tomorrow, Mimi?" (I could tell he was looking forward to the drive and to seeing his good friend Brian again. He had already packed his bag for the weekend, and put it in the boot leaving space for mine.)

"Just going to pack now Dad, and don't worry if you thought the oil was low because the fairies have sprinkled fairy dust everywhere so the engine is in a great condition!"

"Well actually," he said, "the oil was low and I was going to top it up before we started off, but if the fairies have done it," he paused to look at the oil level, "then I have no need to do it myself, do I?" He smiled, gave the motor a quick polish with a rag, and then slammed the bonnet shut.

Forget-me-not wanted to go in the plywood hotel with the tiny fairies. "I don't think you can," I said, "because the hotel is not adapted for your size." She looked sad and said she was feeling homesick. Then I had an idea. "Don't worry," I said, "why don't you travel in the matchbox like you did to get here? I have still got the box, and you could fold up in your leaf state like you did before."

"But I was very stiff after making the journey folded up as I was."

"Okay then." I saw her sorry expression and I really wanted to help. "What I think we could do is to put you in a hankie so you will be flat and comfortable and won't need to be folded. I shall put you on my knee while we travel."

"That's a wonderful idea Mimi, but remember to keep me a secret from your Dad. Put me in your pocket instead of your knee; the others at home would never forgive me if I was found out by a grown-up!"

Suddenly Clover and Chive appeared in blossom petal dresses. "It's happened, it's happened, come and see!"

"What's happened?" I asked eagerly.

"What has happened is the owl egg has hatched!" they said in unison. I had forgotten about the owls in the tree with their three eggs. I decided to get Dad's step-ladder and lean it against the tree; then I was going to take a look.

What I found was not just one egg that had hatched but all three of them!

"The other two chicks must have hatched in the last five minutes," Clover said, and then added: "When I looked there were two eggs and one chick."

"Aren't they sweet!" I said, "Mum owl and Dad owl are very proud." The babies hardly had any feathers and had their beaks open ready for food. All the fairies were flying around the nest, chattering excitedly amongst themselves.

"It's getting late," I said, "the car has a full tank of petrol ready for the journey tomorrow."

Then, I saw the Fairy Queen come outside of the kingdom. She called to all her tiny fairies telling them to come inside and to save their magic dust for the weekend away.

"See you tomorrow, Mimi," said Buttercup.

Chapter Eleven

THE NEXT DAY I was up at six o'clock which was very early for me. I went into the garden and saw that the fairies were already waiting for me in the plywood hotel. I could see them dressed in primrose petals sitting on the tiny pebbles busy talking about leaf fairies and their abilities to change from fairies to leaves.

"It's not just an ability," one fairy said.

"I know," said another, "it is a gift."

Then one more said: "With our magic dust we can cast spells, but we don't store it in tree trunks like leaf fairies do."

Buttercup then said, "Part of our reason for this trip is to find out from the leaf fairies what the freesias are for. I can't wait to see another fairy kingdom set up in a different way."

Dad put the hotel on the back seat of the car and I sat in the front passenger seat. By eight-thirty we were ready to go, including Forget-me-not who was wrapped in a hankie in my pocket. Mum stood outside waving as we set off and we waved back at her until we'd turned a corner and she was out of sight. Dad drove moderately slowly because I told him the fairies don't like being bounced along. When we arrived, Flufftuff greeted us with sloppy kisses, tail wagging and jumping up as usual. Dad went inside to chat to Brian and I decided to look around the garden. I saw the great big tree by the pond with its branches stretching over the water.

So, this is the Leaf-fairy-food-tree, I thought to myself. I took my hankie out of my pocket and carefully unwrapped Forget-me-not. Suddenly I was surrounded by ten or twelve leaf fairies. They were all so pretty, just like the fairy pictures I had seen in Aunt Florence's books. Their dresses were made out of material, and there were feathers and beads around their necks. They wore soft leather sandals decorated with tiny shells. Each one had a different hairstyle; either worn up in a head scarf or long with ribbons, all different colours. Lavender had long flowing curls which trailed all the way down her back. She had the same purple wings as Forget-me-not which was probably why they were close friends.

They sat together by the pond for ages, catching up with each other's news. Chive of course was the only tiny fairy that had been here before. It was all new and exciting for the others. Together they explored every corner of Brian's garden, looking at all the healthy plants that the leaf fairies obviously looked after so well.

When night came, the leaf fairies flew up to the hole in the tree trunk and disappeared from view. The tiny fairies were happy in their plywood hotel and soon went to sleep. I was in Brian's spare room, my bed near the window so I could hear the rain as it came down. At least Buttercup,

Primrose, Honeysuckle, Chive and Clover will be dry, I thought to myself.

When I woke up I felt a tickle on my nose again. "Mimi, it's me, Buttercup. All the fairies are up already. We have been told by a leaf fairy called 'Daisy' that we can go and look inside the Leaf-fairy-food-tree today." I got dressed and went downstairs.

"Woof woof!" Flufftuff got up when he saw me.

"Shhh!" I said. I didn't want him to wake up Dad or Brian.

I went outside and looked up at the big fairy tree. The tiny fairies were all dressed in yellow-coloured primrose dresses today. They were all dancing in the sunlight.

"This way," said a leaf fairy with pale pink wings. She guided the tiny fairies up to the top of the tree trunk where the entrance was. Buttercup said she'd tell me everything when she came out.

"Okay then," I said, "bye, good luck!"

I waited and waited and soon got bored. Dad and Brian eventually surfaced and decided to go for a cycle ride. They knew I was content enough by myself. Of course I wasn't really by myself and it was so magical to be in a different fairy kingdom.

During the night Forget-me-not and Lavender had sprinkled magic dust over Dad's and Brian's heads. I was told that they did this so that they would forget all about the fairies completely. Forget-me-not said that it wasn't right for adults to know about any fairies, whether they are big or small. I promised not to talk about them anymore to any grown-up.

After about an hour, I saw the tiny fairies fly out from the hole in the tree trunk.

"Mimi, Mimi," said Buttercup, "the leaf fairies keep their magic dust in a huge jar inside the tree!"

"Yes I know because Forget-me-not told me about it," I replied.

"The jar," she continued, "is at the base of the tree trunk and is a brilliant white colour. The magic dust is quite like ours which we keep in a pile behind the rockery. I saw the sparkly box with the notepad and flowers inside. It was just like Forget-me-not described—amazingly fresh freesias kept inside a dark box. They have been there for years but never die."

"What else was in there?" I asked.

"In the box, you mean?"

"Yes."

"Nothing else, just a notepad as I said."

I wondered to myself what the leaf fairies had been wondering for so long; why were these fresh flowers there? Was it just to make the air in the tree trunk smell sweet? Did a person put them there or maybe a fairy cast a magic spell to put them there, I wondered?

For the rest of the weekend I spent time talking to different leaf fairies and my tiny fairies (who were enjoying their holiday immensely). I was very fond of my tiny fairies who still thought of me as *sweet girl of the rockery*.

When we got home, the Fairy Queen (who had not been on the trip) asked Honeysuckle and the others if they had taken a step further to establishing why the freesias were in the leaf-fairy-food-tree.

"No we didn't," said Honeysuckle.

"We still don't know," said Primrose.

"We will find out one day," said Buttercup.

Chapter Twelve

IT WAS TEN YEARS LATER. I had moved out of
home into my own flat in the city. I had a job in a bank
where I had worked for one year now. I still visited Mum
and Dad at the weekends, and when I did I always had a
fairy by my side as I walked in the woods.

Over the years, many more fairies had been made from
daisies, and I couldn't keep up with who was new and who
wasn't. Whenever I spend a night at Mum and Dad's, my
favourite fairies stay near me. Honeysuckle, Buttercup,
Primrose, Clover and Chive are with me when I fall asleep
and there for me when I wake up. They are always so
cheerful, nimble and perky.

One particular weekend, Buttercup and the others
gathered around me in blossom dresses and sang:

> *"We have a fairy,*
> *We call him a sprite*
> *We can't see his wings*

He came here tonight,
He's new to the kingdom,
That's why we all sing,
We're happy together,
And that's a great thing."

To me he looked as agile and lively as the other tiny fairies; the only differences were that firstly he was a 'he' and secondly he kept his wings under his clothes.

"I can just see him," I said to Buttercup. "Can't you sprinkle some magic dust on him and make him bigger?" I asked.

"You mean can I cast a spell on him?" said Buttercup.

Then, Primrose tried to explain that being made bigger wasn't always right for the tiny fairies so it may be wrong for the Sprite. She said, "What if he cries when he is not with anyone else anymore his size?"

"Well," I said, "let Buttercup cast the spell on the Sprite *and you too*. Is that okay with you Primrose?"

She thought about it for a minute and then nodded, saying to me, "Okay Mimi, this could be fun." She sounded a little shaky though.

"Don't worry," said Chive, "we have many more spells from our Fairy Queen including a spell to bring you back from a big fairy to your usual tiny self."

It was reassuring for Primrose to hear this, as she was getting quite anxious about it all.

"Count to three!" said Buttercup, holding her bag of

fairy dust ready to throw it over them. Everyone including Lucky stood very still, watching, waiting to see what would happen. There was no sound at all apart from a bird in the sky suddenly flying to a different tree. I saw Buttercup sprinkle the magic dust, and then I held my breath as she said, "One, two, three!"

All the tiny fairies sat on the soft moss as still as statues. Then very gradually I began to see a shape of a boy in front of me. He was just like an elf; green suede jumper and trousers, a green velvet hat with a feather on it and beautifully made leather boots. He also had a sparkling belt which shone in the sun.

"I am the first Sprite ever," he said.

"What shall we call you?" asked a fairy called Jasmine.

"I shall take the first letter of your name and give myself the name 'Jaunty', okay?"

"Yes, yes okay," all the fairies said in unison. Then Primrose appeared—the same size as Jaunty. "Hello, my name is Primrose," she said introducing herself, feeling that this was the next logical thing to say. "I am one of the rockery fairies, and very pleased to meet you." They shook hands and hugged.

"It's amazing," she said to me, "being so big, you know; I can now go into the house by opening the back door instead of flying through an open gap in the middle of the window or beneath the door."

"Is that what you had to do to get into the house before?" Jaunty asked.

I had a thought, and interrupted them because I thought it necessary. "Jaunty and Primrose, it really would not be a good idea to go into the house as big as you both are because you might get caught. Jaunty might get away with it, but not you, Primrose, with your wings on display. The thing is that you would have to explain yourselves and that would be difficult."

"We must live in the woods today," said Jaunty, "and then come back in the evening and have the spell reversed so we can spend the night in the kingdom."

"Yes," said Primrose, "let's go and enjoy ourselves."

They looked at me and I realised they wanted me to come too.

"Please Mimi!" said Primrose. I could not refuse and was still taken aback at the powers of the magic dust. Holding each other's hands, we set off for the woods.

"How do you know you are the only Sprite in the world?" I asked.

"Because the Fairy Queen made a wish one day by using her wand, to have a male fairy because she was getting bored with female fairies coming to her for stories or magic spells or holly berry juice. She felt she needed someone for herself, who could help her feel happier and joyous, and who could spend the day laughing and joking at her side."

"The last time I saw the Fairy Queen was way back

when I was ten," I said. "We had just returned from a few days away at my Dad's friends' house." I continued: "I am not surprised that she was able to make you from a spell. I wonder what words she used?"

"Maybe she used 'freesia' in her spell," suggested Primrose.

"It could be that she did, yes," I said, "that would make some sense about why the freesias were in the Leaf-fairy-food-tree. It could be, but I'm not sure, that Buttercup was needed to tell the Fairy Queen about the Leaf fairies' tree with the box of freesias in it. Until the Fairy Queen knew about this, she could not cast a spell to make a sprite come to the kingdom." I felt very confident about my theory.

As we walked along the path it became muddy and slippery. A dog ran up to us so we knew there were people ahead. I wasn't worried though because Jaunty and Primrose looked like they were my children and that we were on a family walk. I took off my coat and put it on Primrose so her wings could not be seen. The coat was a long one, and covered her lovely dress, which to others probably looked over the top for a country walk. If anyone asked why the children were dressed like this, I decided I would say that they had just come back from a fancy-dress party. When we walked past the dog's owners, they both nodded to me and said hello. Nothing else was said and we went our separate ways.

I noticed that Jaunty and Primrose were not scared of other people; in fact, they were the opposite. If people acknowledged them, then they would return the attention by nodding back and smiling. I thought to myself that it must be so refreshing to see other human beings instead of all the same fairies day in and day out. And to be a different size, well, I considered that too; what wonderful magic it all was.

"What's important," Jaunty suddenly said, "is that we find some stinging nettles that are any colour but green."

"Why?" Primrose asked.

"Because the Fairy Queen explained to me that she needed nettles for renovating part of the kingdom. Any cracks or leaks inside, she said, are mended with stinging nettles."

"It's easier for *us* to collect them because we have gloves," said Primrose, "and being this big we can carry many more, can't we, Mimi?"

I smiled at her, but was still curious about why the nettles must not be green. I decided to wait until we took a rest at the brow of the hill and then ask him. We sat on an old tree stump and I took a flask out of my bag. When I handed Jaunty a cup of tea I said, "There's no such thing as blue, pink, yellow or purple nettles!"

He said, "The Fairy Queen told me she had cast a spell last night to change the colour of some nettles so we would see them and not miss any. Only the biggest and strongest will stand out and we will know by their different colours which ones to pick."

"Oh, I see," I said, feeling pleased that they were talking to me about it.

"Look!" Jaunty shouted, pointing to one of the hedges. I

stooped down to his level and I could just see something very luminous and yellow, which I'd never seen before. I thought that this had to be one of the coloured nettles and I was right. Primrose leant into the hedge and picked loads of nettles while singing merrily to herself. Jaunty beat away the brambles with a stick so they could reach more of them.

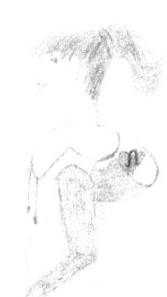

"It's getting dark," said Primrose as she fastened her rucksack. There were two robins on the ground jumping along in front of us.

"Stop," I said, "are any tiny rockery fairies here?"

"Yes," said a little voice, "I have been sitting in your coat hood all day!"

Quickly I took off my coat and examined the inside. I took the magnifying glass out of my pocket and put it up to my eye. I hadn't seen her before and I was amazed at her dress. It had rosemary leaves sewn into the seams and little violet flowers dotted all over it. I asked her what her name was, and she replied:

"My name is Violet. I keep myself busy by sewing herbs into my dresses. They can be used as a perfume, and that's the reason I've picked this herb to wear; I love the smell of all herbs. I wish I could come with you, Mimi, back to your flat in the city!"

This was a strange thing to say, I thought to myself; maybe she was lonely. Then, she started to cry, and I watched as big tears rolled down her cheeks. Even though she was so tiny, as I was looking at her through the magnifying glass I could still see her upset face. I asked her what was wrong and she said:

"It's the same thing day in and day out. I sew and I sew and I sew, and I don't ever do anything different. I get so bored in the kingdom and that's why I stowed away with you today, just to have a change."

When we got back, the Fairy Queen was waiting outside for us. She smiled and made a remark about how the weather had been nice today. Next she looked at the two giant fairies and said:

"Primrose and Jaunty, my dears, let's change you back to your normal sizes so I can hug you both."

She scattered magic dust into the air, and I watched them be transformed back to tiny sized fairies again.

"Jaunty," she said, "come to the kingdom and drink some holly berry juice with me in my quarters. Primrose, darling, Buttercup, Clover and Chive are waiting for you inside. There's holly berry juice and food laid out on a table for you."

"Did you notice someone missing today?" I asked, then added: "Violet has been with us, you know."

"Well actually," said the Fairy Queen, "I had noticed she had gone, but she does often go into the garden amongst the herbs by herself."

"She gets so bored," I said.

The Fairy Queen breathed a big sigh, and told me that every day there was at least one fairy complaining about being bored. She said that having Jaunty in the kingdom should stop anyone getting bored because he was always around to talk to.

Part 2

Chapter Thirteen

HELLO, I'M HONEYSUCKLE, and I am one of Mimi's favourite fairies.

The story of the china plate was still interesting to me and I can imagine how it came to be. I learnt how Mimi's friends' dog knocked over the plate on the coffee table, and that it shattered into tiny pieces. Then, Primrose and Buttercup had asked Mimi if they could keep a piece and bring it inside the kingdom. It had pride of place in the hall and was apparently to celebrate the uncovering of the kingdom door. I'd often ask Buttercup what they were celebrating that day, and she'd reply, "Honeysuckle, let me explain; Mimi had uncovered our fairy door that day by using a trowel to dig away all the rabbit droppings."

I knew Mimi was here this weekend and that she was walking in the woods today with Jaunty and Primrose. I decided to wait outside because I wanted to have another look at how large they were. When I got outside, the Fairy Queen had already cast her spell, and they were their usual sizes again. Buttercup looked at me and said:

"Violet has been out all day too! She's been in Mimi's hood!"

Violet blushed and said, "I just couldn't stand another day inside doing the same thing."

I knew she was one of the fairies who were always complaining to the Fairy Queen of being bored. I didn't dare say that because I loved everything about each fairy.

Next, we all went inside to have a meal and drink some holly berry juice. Afterwards I helped to bring in the luminous stinging nettles and put them in a heap by the quartz tables.

I woke up early the next day. I went outside of the kingdom and saw Lucky scampering after a vole. Now in her later years, she wasn't as fast as she used to be. She had a few white hairs around her nose and incorporated into her black fur.

"Honeysuckle, can you help us make a bracelet for Mimi? She's going back to her flat today."

Buttercup was always asking me to do some sort of a favour. I think she feels protective over me because I am just a little bit younger than her.

"Okay," I said, "I'll help."

The other day she had asked me to spray lots of primrose and blossom dresses and the day before that, she had asked me to polish all the tables. The dresses were sprayed with fragrance and a cleaning solution; they were not washed because that would ruin them.

As I went over to the other fairies, I could hear their excitable voices. The Fairy Queen appeared and there was a hush, as everyone went quiet.

"Now," she said, "each fairy must take one bead off her necklace and put it on the ground. When all the beads are sewn together I will cast my spell. Firstly they must be sewn together, so, the lucky fairy that has this to do is…" I waited hoping she would say my name.

"Violet!"

I gave a sigh of disappointment, but that feeling soon went as we all clapped and cheered Violet. Everyone chose a bead from their necklaces; mine was an amber colour.

I wondered how much time we had before Mimi left. "Well," said Clover, "Chive has flown into Mimi's bedroom, and will give us a sign when Mimi is packing to leave. She always leaves her packing to the last minute, and then drives home immediately after that."

I looked up to Mimi's bedroom window and saw her looking out at us. "We can see her," I said. "but she can't see us!"

"I think she's coming now," said the Fairy Queen. "Chive is flying over to us."

Violet looked a bit worried. "I'm not ready yet," she said. "Honeysuckle, can you help me by flying around this cotton reel with the end of the cotton in your hands?"

Mimi had once given us the cotton, years ago, and we had used it for several things; it was always needed for new dresses. I flew around it until we had enough for the bracelet. Violet threaded all the beads together and then it was ready. We all stood back as the Fairy Queen cast her spell:

"Make this bracelet as big as can be
It's to fit the wrist of Mimi."

There was a bright flash and we all opened our eyes and saw a pretty bracelet shining and glistening in the sun.

"Thank-you everyone for giving a bead," said the Fairy Queen. "If it wasn't for Mimi, then lots of good things here wouldn't have happened, so, this is a thank-you present."

Next, Mimi walked over to the golden doorway, expecting to see us all to say bye-bye. We all flew over to the moss next to the door. I flew up to her shoulder with Primrose and Buttercup.

"Mimi, there's something special on your car that is a present from us all," I said.

We all flew over to Mimi's car and waited for her to walk there. As soon as she saw the bracelet on the bonnet her face lit up. "Where on earth did you get this from?" she asked.

"We made it ourselves!" said Buttercup to Mimi, adding; "You are still my best friend sweet girl of the rockery; you deserve this present. Will you wear it all the time?"

Mimi smiled and held out her hand for Buttercup to land on. She had tears in her eyes and she was trembling. She said to Buttercup:

"If only I could stay here all the time, but now I have a job so I have to stay in my flat all week without seeing any of you."

"Why can't you get a job here in the village and stay with your mum and dad instead?" I asked.

"Because, Honeysuckle, I am too old to stay at home with Mum and Dad. They don't know much about you; actually they think my interest in fairies was just a childhood fad. They would think I was strange if I lived with them again and spent all day in the garden talking to you all. In fact they would think I was talking to myself and worry I was ill."

I watched as she put on the bracelet with my amber bead in the middle. She looked at me and Buttercup and said, "This is lovely! Thank-you so much! I will wear it all the time and think of you when I look at it. Now, I must go to the city but I will be back next weekend. The daisies are up so there might be a new fairy by the time I'm back. Take care everyone, bye!"

She drove off leaving me feeling sad. "I will miss her Jaunty," I said to the Sprite who was next to me.

"Come on, let's have some fun," he said; then he took my hand and we flew up high into the sky, twisting and turning in the air.

Chapter Fourteen

THE NEXT MORNING I awoke later than everyone else. There are not separate bedrooms for each of us in the kingdom; there is just one large room with three hundred and seventy six beds in it which is the number of fairies there is. Where is everyone, I thought to myself? Why had I slept longer than everyone else? I got dressed quickly, fixed my hair and decided to find out what was going on.

I found Clover polishing the quartz tables and chairs. "Why is everyone up earlier than I am?" I asked her.

"I don't know," she replied, "it's probably because they weren't as tired as you were. No one else went flying with Jaunty all evening. All that fresh air and exercise is bound to make you sleepy. We have all been doing our usual thing."

Suddenly I remembered that I was one of the ten fairies who had been chosen to sit under a daisy and talk to each other. I told Clover but she said that this was happening tomorrow, not today.

"Why don't you find something else to do like helping me polish?" she suggested.

I always admired how Clover stayed so chirpy whatever the weather, whatever the day. As I polished I started thinking about Jaunty and how much I liked him. He was every fairy's dream sprite, so handsome and quirky. I imagined us scattering magic dust together, laughing and having fun at the same time.

The mirror needed polishing so I started cleaning it and then looked at my reflection. I forgot what I was meant to be doing, put the duster down and began to fiddle with my hair. I stared at my face—it was quite a nice looking face really. My eyes were a sky blue colour and I had a really wide smile. My hair was curly and very long, and my wings fragile and pretty. Would Jaunty choose me out of all the beautiful fairies to be his girlfriend? He did seem to enjoy himself when we were together. I sighed and looked down.

"What are you thinking about?" Clover had noticed I had stopped dusting.

"Oh Clover," I said, "I was miles away." I decided to finish dusting and go to the rest room.

The kingdom's rest room is by far the most glamorous of all the rooms. There is silver tinsel all over the ceiling and sparkly tiles on the walls. I have a special place that I like the most which is in the middle of the room where there are several reclining chairs. I always sit there and today was no different, except for one thing—Jaunty was lying on my chair! He was snoozing away in the land of nod. I was about to walk away, but I decided first I shall go and have a closer look. I crept quietly up to him, and leaned over him, watching I didn't fall over.

Suddenly he opened his eyes, and was so surprised to see me that he fell off the chair!

"Honeysuckle!"

"I didn't mean to wake you," I said, then added, "I just wanted to look at you." I blushed.

"That's alright," he smiled. "I was catching up on my sleep; we were out so late last night!"

While listening to him and smiling I had an urge to kiss him.

"Well, Honeysuckle, would you…"

Before he could finish his sentence I kissed him on his cheek. Then I said with my hands to my mouth, "I'm sorry," and blushing again I turned towards the door.

"Don't go," he said, "I love you, Honeysuckle, oops… I've said it now! I don't think you love me though, do you?"

I couldn't believe he loved me out of all the three hundred and seventy six of us. I wanted to be sure he meant it so I said:

"Am I the only one you love?"

"Yes you are. I like the rest of the fairies but I don't love them."

"Oh," I said, "Well, let's tell everyone that we are together… er…" (I was a bit worried that if we kept our love a secret, then some of the others might think they had a chance with Jaunty.)

"It's okay, Honeysuckle," he said, adding, "If we get married you will feel more secure. I've only got eyes for you anyway."

I grinned at him thinking about how my friends would react when they knew the news.

"Should we tell the Fairy Queen that we are going to get married, Jaunty?"

"Umm," he thought out loud, "Yes, because it is only with her special magic consent that the dream can come true. Let's go to her now."

I felt so special walking next to Jaunty, holding his hand. We reached the Fairy Queen's room and waited patiently for her to answer our call. I sprinkled magic dust on the floor as a sign of respect, and then she appeared.

"My dears, how lovely to see you both," she smiled. "I have great news to tell!"

"So have we!" said Jaunty.

I wondered what the Fairy Queen's news could be, and thought we should hold onto our news until after she had told us hers. I bowed my head and looked at her graciously.

"I'd love to know your news," said Jaunty, folding his arms and smiling.

"Me too," I said.

"Come into my room and meet three new sprites for the kingdom!"

Chapter Fifteen

WHEN I LOOKED at the three sprites in front of us, I clapped my hands and said:

"Maybe three fairies will be happy to have a sprite each."

The Fairy Queen said, "Each sprite will find a fairy to love and then will get married. I can see that"—looking at Jaunty and myself—"you two love each other, am I right?"

"Oh, you are very right!" said Jaunty who was looking fondly at me.

"I believe you are right for each other," she said. "When Mimi comes home," continued the Fairy Queen, "I will ask her to take off her bracelet and then I will touch the amber stone of yours, Honeysuckle. Then you both kiss the stone because that is how fairies and sprites marry. There's no ceremony or cake or rings unless Mimi gets married herself. Then, if she does, then the fairy and sprite weddings can happen."

I said goodbye and left the Fairy Queen's quarters, full of anticipation.

The next day there was no boredom amongst the fairies at all. They all crowded around the three new sprites, each trying to see what they looked like.

"What are your names?" asked Violet, raising her voice and standing on a chair.

"My name is Tim," said one sprite, and then he added, "And this is Michael and Robin."

Everyone went quiet as the Fairy Queen made an appearance. "Settle down everyone," she said. "Now this really is the limit. I have no more spells to make any more sprites. I have used magic to have them here but the spell could only be used four times. Unfortunately this means that the most of you will not have your own sprite. There is only Jaunty who is Honeysuckle's, Michael, Robin and Tim." She showered us all with Fairy dust and then went inside.

"So how do we know which is which?" asked Buttercup.

"By our differences, like how you tell each other apart," said one.

"Are you all different ages?" asked Primrose.

"Yes, Michael is the oldest, Robin is in the middle and Tim is the youngest," said another.

"Do you drink holly berry juice?" asked Clover.

"Yes," said the third one, "we drink it like you do."

I watched as all the fairies were questioning the sprites at the same time.

"Shhhhh," I said.

"No Honeysuckle, we will not be quiet!" It was Chive who spoke. "What's wrong with finding things out from our new arrivals?" she asked me.

I thought about it and then said: "You must not interrogate the sprites by bombarding them with questions! Let them join in with you on the rockery. I'm sure that they would like to know what herb is what and to fly about the garden. Jaunty and I are getting married as soon as Mimi returns, but this doesn't mean that the three new sprites have to choose a fairy to marry by then. Have fun with each other, cast spells and play games; get to know each other." Having said this, I took a deep breath and stopped talking.

"Honeysuckle is right!"

"Yes, we shouldn't ask so many questions."

"We should celebrate really!"

"Life won't be boring anymore!"

"Let's show Michael, Robin and Tim all around the rockery."

"Yes, and let's introduce Lucky to them."

I smiled to myself as I saw the fairies talk excitably to each other about how their lives would change. I knew mine certainly would, as soon as Mimi returned.

The next weekend she arrived earlier than usual on the Friday afternoon. She got out of the car and went inside the house. We followed her inside but were careful not to be seen by her mum and dad. I watched with the others as she said:

"Mum, Dad, I've got some wonderful news!"

"Oh, what's that?" her dad asked.

"I've got engaged! He works at the bank too; we've been friends for years and he is called John."

I felt a lump in my throat as I heard her words. If she was going to get married, then Jaunty and I would be able to share her ceremony. It would mean that we could have a party! I clapped my hands and all the others clapped too.

I wondered what Mimi might say when I told her my news. I waited outside for her. After a couple of hours she eventually came out. She sat on a big stone covered in moss. We all danced around her in our blossom petal dresses.

"It's lovely to see you sweet girl of the rockery," Buttercup said to Mimi.

"It's lovely to see you all dancing," she replied.

We sprinkled fairy dust on the grass and it sparkled like diamonds. We asked her if she still had her bracelet on; she nodded and showed us all.

"We must kiss your amber stone, Mimi," said Jaunty.

"Why?" she asked.

"Because that's how Honeysuckle and I can marry."

"Oh, is that right?" she said, looking at us.

"Yes, the Fairy Queen told us to do this," I said.

"Alright then, Honeysuckle and Jaunty." She held out her arm and we flew over to the bracelet. We kissed the amber stone so we were then married.

"I'm getting married too," said Mimi. She smiled and I

jumped up and down with joy. "Can Jaunty and me come to your wedding and celebrate our marriage too?"

"Of course you can," smiled Mimi, "but I don't know when it will be."

I felt so happy I could cry. However, I held back the tears and danced with Clover and Chive instead.

"With all that has gone on over the week we haven't had time to sit under a listening daisy to make a new fairy!" exclaimed Clover.

Part 3

Chapter Sixteen

THAT NIGHT I lay awake, thinking how happy Jaunty and Honeysuckle seemed now they were married. I thought of my dear John in the city, soon to be my husband. I closed my eyes and went to sleep with a smile on my face. My dreams were of fairies and sprites, and when I woke up there were fairies all around me.

"Did you sleep well, sweet girl of the rockery? It's me, Buttercup, your best friend."

"Yes I did," I said, yawning and stretching. "Is it really true that the kingdom has four sprites inside now?"

"Yes Mimi," said Buttercup, "there's Jaunty, Michael, Robin and Tim."

I had met Jaunty and spent time with him last weekend with Primrose, but I hadn't yet seen the other three. I thought out of all the fairies that Violet was the most deserving to marry one of the sprites. She had really touched a nerve the day she stowed away in my hood. She was beautiful in her dress with rosemary and violet flowers sewn into it. I had seen her cry because she felt so lonely.

"Has Violet met the sprites?" I asked Buttercup.

"Yes, we all have," she replied.

What I didn't know was that all the sprites were trying to renovate the bad patches of the kingdom with the stinging nettles we had collected.

"Can I meet them today?" I asked,

"Oh, I don't know Mimi," said Buttercup, adding: "They are kind of busy all day today but when they stop for a break, I'll tell them you are in the garden and that you would like to see them. Is that okay?"

"Yes Buttercup, that's fine."

Buttercup flew away and I went inside. I sat on my bed and began thinking about Forget-me-not. It seemed such a long time ago that she lived with me in this bedroom. I always knew that she would eventually return to her real home in Brian's garden. Leaf fairies can't survive without their food from the leaf-fairy-food-tree and there was only holly berry juice here for the tiny fairies.

Forget-me-not went home with Brian one day to re-join Lavender and the other leaf fairies. Now I wished she was here, to listen to me and tell me of her adventures with the rockery fairies. I sighed and closed my eyes. I could picture Forget-me-not in her lovely purple dress, singing and dancing and gracefully flapping her wings. I smiled and a big tear rolled down my cheek.

When I opened my eyes I looked at the clock to see that an hour had passed. I must have fallen asleep! I put a jumper on because it was quite cold and looked out of the window. I wished in my heart that the fairies weren't so tiny, so I could see them better. Then, I left my bedroom and went downstairs and out into the garden. I took the magnifying glass with me so I'd be able to see the sprites in detail. When I got to the kingdom's golden door, Lucky brushed up against me. I noticed two dead voles which she had caught earlier on. I stroked her and said, "Have you seen any fairies today?" I then laughed at myself; fancy talking to an animal who cannot understand what I say! Lucky looked at me though as if she did understand. She walked away from me, then turned round and meowed. She stood still until I came up to her, and then she led me up the rockery to a lavender plant. She sniffed at the grass next to it and looked up at me. I bent down and took out the magnifying glass and looked at the grass. In between the blades of grass and resting on a little stone were Michael, Robin and Tim.

"Hello," I said, "will you all be at Honeysuckle's and Jaunty's and my wedding party?"

"Yes," they all chorused together. Tim flew up onto my shoulder and said in my ear: "I was hoping I'd see you this morning. I waited outside the back door for you. Then Mimi, when you didn't come out, I went back to my bedroom in the kingdom where Michael and Robin were. We have heard all about you and how you look after the fairies of the rockery." Tim was the smallest of the sprites, and very endearing I thought. Robin was a bit bigger, and Michael was the biggest. Next, Michael flew onto my shoulder, his wings tickling my neck. Instantly I felt he would be my friend. Then Voilet and Buttercup flew up to me and landed next to Michael and Tim.

"Hello Tim, I'm Violet."

"You are so pretty."

"Well, it's because I take care of my hair and skin and choose nice clothes to wear."

"Did you make this beautiful dress?"

"Yes I did. Did you make your trousers and pullover?"

"No, the Fairy Queen cast a spell, that I would be dressed like this right from the beginning."

As they kept talking, I walked away to let them be, hoping they would continue to get along so well. Robin and Michael came with me as I went to get a deckchair from the shed. I sat down to think about my own wedding and decided that when I got back to the city I would start to make plans.

Chapter Seventeen

A **YEAR LATER**, the wedding day eventually arrived. Mum and Dad had helped me with all the plans; we had been very busy arranging it all. Everything had come together, from the colour of the bridesmaids' dresses to the number of tiers on the wedding cake. I had racked my brains about how to invite the two fairies and their sprites so they could be bigger for the day but not recognised as fairies. Honeysuckle and Violet and their partners, Jaunty and Tim, wanted so much to look like children at the wedding so they could join in with the real children there. If they stayed tiny then they would not be noticed and it would be miserable for them. So, I asked the Fairy Queen if she could cast a spell, like she did on Jaunty and Primrose the day we went to the woods. She had agreed, much to the delight of the two couples. Although they were already married by kissing the amber stone on my bracelet, my wedding was the chance for them to really celebrate.

I was so nervous because today was the day. "Let me help you with that," Mum said as she saw me struggling to zip up the back of my dress.

"Thanks Mum," I said and then added, "What a coincidence that my cousin's birthday is today. Will he be bringing any friends to the reception?"

"Actually Mimi," Mum said, "yes, he will be. Two girls and two boys who I have not met are coming."

I smiled at Mum and said, "Good, that will be nice."

I had asked my cousin a few weeks ago if he would pretend that Jaunty, Tim, Honeysuckle and Violet were his friends. He was only eight but very grown up for his age. It would be wonderful to see the fairies his size today.

I finished my make-up and started on my hair. I had a friend to help me. She said: "We must hurry up because we have to be at the church by eleven, and it's ten o'clock now!"

"The car will be around very soon," Mum said. "Dad will be there and John is already on his way to the church with Peter." (Peter was John's best man.) I still felt so excited about getting married to my John who was so lovely.

"Okay, Mum. I'm very nervous!"

"You will be fine. I will see you at the church. You will always be my little girl even when you are married." I took a big breath and sighed. Mum had always made sure everything went alright, whatever it might be. I shouted: "Today is going to be the best day of my life!"

My friend Mary laughed and said, "You look lovely. Let

me fix the veil for you." She pinned it carefully onto the tiara I had taken so much time to choose. "Now," she said, "You have something old and something new, but not something borrowed or blue." She was right; I had an old button sewed onto the lining of my dress, and the dress itself was brand new. I checked the button was still in place and then looked up at Mary. "Here, this is for you," she said, handing me a very delicate blue bracelet. "You can have it, and you can borrow this hankie too!"

Now I was all set up, and before I had time to worry about anything, the car drove up outside. I looked out of the window to see Dad get out of the car smiling at me and very smart in his new suit. "You look amazing Mimi!" he said as he stepped inside. We piled into the car—me, Dad, Mum and Mary who was my bridesmaid. She was wearing a purple fitted dress with white lace at the neckline and cuffs. My dress was very long and made from silk and shimmered in the light. Getting out of the car I was careful not to dirty any part of my dress. I walked into the church with Dad by my side, holding me steady as I took little steps in my high heels.

Before I knew it, the ceremony was over and we were outside again having photos taken. Everyone was smiling and chatting to each other, and throwing confetti. I took John's hand and he put his arms around me and then we walked through the churchyard to the church hall. All our friends and family followed, and soon the hall was packed. I spotted the fairies after I had eaten some sandwiches from the buffet. They were filling their plates with chicken drumsticks and coleslaw. Their wings were hidden under their clothes and they just looked like any normal children.

"This is your time to party too," I whispered to Honeysuckle and Violet when no one else was in earshot.

"Oh, we are so happy today!" said Violet. "Just think about it—a few weeks ago we found everything so boring and mundane, but now, Honeysuckle and I are married to two perfect partners—Jaunty and Tim!"

"We are going to just blend in with the crowd," Tim said to me.

"That's right," I said, "don't give anything away, will you?"

"No, of course not," said Honeysuckle while looking at Jaunty. I could see she was smitten by him.

The band started to play and lots of people started to dance.

"Your cousins are very nimble and perky," said one guest to me as she watched the fairies and sprites dance with one another. "Oh," I said blushing, "only one of them is my cousin, and he's always been very agile and spirited. The other children are just his friends."

"Well, they all look very spritely," she said. I blushed again and turned away before my face got even redder. If only she knew, I thought to myself!

Next, Brian was in front of me. "Congratulations to the both of you!" He kissed me and shook John's hand. "You know John," he said, "I have watched this girl grow up from a baby to a child, to a teenager to an adult. As I don't have children of my own, I have doted on her as if she were my own daughter. Please look after her and take care of her because she is yours now and not mine anymore."

He patted John on the back and returned to his table with the other guests. Dad topped up my glass and said that it was time to cut the cake. I could see the fairies and sprites at the front of the crowd watching with joy as they held each other's hands. After the cake had been cut up into little pieces everyone was given a bit. The whole day was a success, and I knew this by everybody's happy expression. Each guest that I spoke to in turn wished us all the happiness in the world. We had many wonderful presents to keep and treasure for ever. But the thing I shall treasure the most is the bracelet the fairies made for me.

The evening went extremely well, I thought as I watched the other two newlywed couples dance the night away. I kept it a secret that this wedding party was not only mine and John's, but Honeysuckle and Jaunty's, and Violet and Tim's too.

This is a day I shall always remember. The magic of the tiny fairies, the sprites and the leaf-fairies will live on forever.